# NATURE MYTHS AND STORIES FOR LITTLE CHILDREN

by

FLORA J. COOKE

# NATURE MYTHS

## AND

## STORIES

### FOR LITTLE CHILDREN

BY
FLORA J. COOKE
of the
Cook County Normal School
Chicago

# PREFACE.

EELING the great need of stories founded upon good literature, which are within the comprehension of little children, I have written the following stories, hoping that they may suggest to primary teachers the great wealth of material within our reach. Many teachers, who firmly believe that reading should be something more than mere *word-getting* while the child's *reading habit* is forming, are practically helpless without the use of a printing press. We will all agree that myths and fables are usually beautiful truths clothed in fancy, and the dress is almost always simple and transparent.

Who can study these myths and not feel that nature has a new language for him, and that though the tales may be thousands of years old, they are quite as true as they were in the days of Homer. If the trees and the flowers, the clouds and the wind, all tell wonderful stories to the child he has sources of happiness of which no power can deprive him.

And when we consider that here, too, is the key which unlocks so much of the best in art and literature, we feel that we cannot rank too highly the importance of the myth in the primary schoolroom.

For instance the child has been observing, reading, and writing about the sun, the moon, the direction of the wind, the trees, the flowers, or the forces that are acting around him. He has had the songs, poems, and pictures connected with these lessons to further enhance his thought, interest, and observation.

He is now given a beautiful myth. He is not expected to interpret it. It is presented for the same purpose that a good picture is placed before him. He feels its beauty, but does not analyze it.

If, through his observation or something in his experience, he *does see a meaning* in the story he has entered a new world of life and beauty.

Then comes the question to every thoughtful teacher, "Can the repetition of words necessary to the growth of the child's vocabulary be obtained in this way?"

This may be accomplished if the teacher in planning her year's work, sees a close relation between the science, literature, and number work, so that the same words are always recurring, and the interest in each line of work is constant and ever increasing.

The following stories are suggested in the standard books of mythology and poetry, and have been tested and found to be very helpful in the first and third grades. A full list of myths, history stories and fairy tales for the children in the different grades can be found in Emily J. Rice's Course of Study in History and Literature, which can be obtained of A. Flanagan, No. 262 Wabash avenue, Chicago.

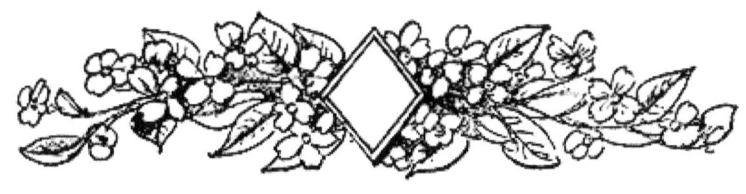

# CONTENTS.

# CLYTIE.

LYTIE was a beautiful little water nymph who lived in a cave at the bottom of the sea. The walls of the cave were covered with pearls and shells. The floor was made of sand as white as snow.

There were many chairs of amber with soft mossy cushions. On each side of the cave-opening was a great forest of coral. Back of the cave were Clytie's gardens.

Here were the sea anemones, starfish and all kinds of seaweed.

In the garden grotto were her horses. These were the gentlest goldfish and turtles.

The ocean fairies loved Clytie and wove her dresses of softest green sea lace.

With all these treasures Clytie should have been happy, but she was not. She had once heard a mermaid sing of a glorious light which shone on the top of the water.

She could think of nothing else, but longed day and night to know more of the wonderful light.

No ocean fairy dared take her to it, and she was afraid to go alone.

One day she was taking her usual ride in her shell carriage. The water was warm and the turtles went so slowly that Clytie soon fell asleep. On and on they went, straight towards the light, until they came to an island.

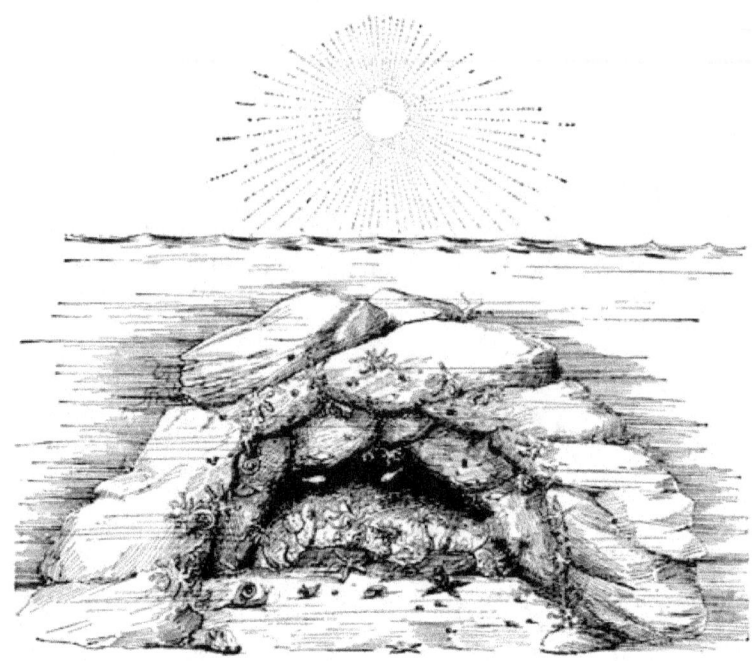

As the waves dashed the carriage against the shore Clytie awoke. She climbed out of the shell and sat down upon a large rock. She had never seen the trees and flowers.

She had never heard the birds chirping or the forest winds sighing.

She had never known the perfume of the flowers or seen the dew on the grass.

In wonder, she saw a little boy and girl near her and heard them say, "Here it comes! Here it comes!"

As she looked away in the east she saw the glorious light that she had so longed for. In its midst, in a golden chariot, sat a wonderful king.

The king smiled and instantly the birds began to sing, the plants unfolded their buds, and even the old sea looked happy.

Clytie sat on the rock all day long and wished that she might be like the great kind king.

She wept when he entered the land of the sunset and she could see him no longer. She went home, but she could scarcely wait until the morning. Very early the next day her swiftest goldfish carried her to the rock.

After this, she came every day, wishing more and more to be like the great kind king. One evening as she was ready to go home, she found that she could not move her feet. She leaned out over the sea and knew that she had her wish. Instead of a water nymph a beautiful sunflower looked back at her from the water.

Her yellow hair had become golden petals, her green lace dress had turned into leaves and stems, and her little feet had become roots which fastened her to the ground.

The good king the next day sent her into many countries, into dry and sandy places, that the people might be made happy by looking at her bright face, so like his own.

# GOLDEN-ROD AND ASTER.

 OLDEN HAIR and Blue Eyes lived at the foot of a great hill.

On the top of this hill in a little hut lived a strange, wise woman.

It was said that she could change people into anything she wished. She looked so grim and severe that people were afraid to go near her.

One summer day the two little girls at the foot of the hill thought they would like to do something to make everybody happy.

"I know," said Golden Hair, "Let us go and ask the woman on the hill about it. She is very wise and can surely tell us just what to do."

"Oh, yes," said Blue Eyes, and away they started at once.

It was a warm day and a long walk to the top of the hill.

The little girls stopped many times to rest under the oak trees which shaded their pathway.

They could find no flowers, but they made a basket of oak leaves and filled it with berries for the wise woman.

They fed the fish in the brook and talked to the squirrels and the birds.

They walked on and on in the rocky path.

After a while the sun went down. The birds stopped singing.

The squirrels went to bed.

The trees fell asleep.

Even the wind was resting.

Oh, how still and cool it was on the hillside!

The moon and stars came out.

The frogs and toads awoke.

The night music began.

The beetles and fireflies flew away to a party.

But the tired little children climbed on towards the hilltop.

At last they reached it.

There at the gate was the strange, old woman, looking even more stern than usual.

The little girls were frightened. They clung close together while brave Golden Hair said, "we know you are wise and we came to see if you would tell us how to make everyone happy."

"Please let us stay together," said timid Blue Eyes.

As she opened the gate for the children, the wise woman was seen to smile in the moonlight. The two little girls were never seen again at the foot of the hill. The next morning all over the hillside people saw beautiful, waving golden-rod and purple asters growing.

It has been said that these two bright flowers, which grow side by side, could tell the secret, if they would, of what became of the two little girls on that moonlight summer night.

# THE WISE KING AND THE BEE.

 ONG ago there lived in the East the greatest king in the world.

It was believed that no one could ask him a question which he could not answer.

Wise men came from far and near, but they were never able to puzzle King Solomon.

He knew all the trees and plants.

He understood the beasts, fowls and creeping things almost as well as he did people.

The fame of his knowledge spread into all lands. In the south, the great Queen of Sheba heard of the wonderful wisdom of Solomon and said, "I shall test his power for myself."

She picked some clover blossoms from the field and bade a great artist make for her, in wax, flowers, buds and leaves exactly like them.

She was much pleased when they were finished, for she herself could see no difference in the two bunches.

She carried them to the king and said, "Choose, Oh wise king, which are the real flowers?"

At first King Solomon was puzzled, but soon he saw a bee buzzing at the window.

"Ah," said he, "here is one come to help me in my choice. Throw open the window for my friend."

Then the Queen of Sheba bowed her head and said:

"You are indeed a wise king, but I begin to understand your wisdom. I thank you for this lesson."

# KING SOLOMON

# AND THE ANTS.

 NE morning the Queen of Sheba started back to her home in the south. King Solomon and all his court went with her to the gates of the city.

It was a glorious sight.

The king and queen rode upon white horses.

The purple and scarlet coverings of their followers glittered with silver and gold.

The king looked down and saw an ant hill in the path before them.

"See yonder little people," he said, "do you hear what they are saying as they run about so wildly?

"They say, 'Here comes the king, men call wise, and good and great.

'He will trample us under his cruel feet.'"

"They should be proud to die under the feet of such a king," said the queen. "How dare they complain?"

"Not so, Great Queen," replied the king.

He turned his horse aside and all his followers did the same.

When the great company had passed there was the ant hill unharmed in the path.

The Queen said, "Happy indeed, must be your people, wise king. I shall remember the lesson.

"He only is noble and great who cares for the helpless and weak."

# ARACHNE.

RACHNE was a beautiful maiden and the most wonderful weaver that ever lived. Her father was famed throughout the land for his great skill in coloring.

He dyed Arachne's wools in all the colors of the rainbow. People came from miles around to see and admire her work. They all agreed that Queen Athena must have been her teacher. Arachne proudly said that she had never been taught to weave. She said that she would be glad to weave with Athena to see which had the greater skill. In vain her father told her that perhaps Athena, unseen, guided her hand.

Arachne would not listen and would thank no one for her gift, believing only in herself. One day as she was boasting of her skill an old woman came to her. She kindly advised her to accept her rare gift humbly.

"Be thankful that you are so fortunate, Arachne," said she.

"You may give great happiness to others by your beautiful work.

"Queen Athena longs to help you.

"But I warn you. She can do no more for you until you grow unselfish and kind."

Arachne scorned this advice and said again that nothing would please her so much as to weave with Athena.

"If I fail," she said, "I will gladly take the punishment, but Athena is afraid to weave with me."

Then the old woman threw aside her cloak and said, "Athena is here.

"Come, foolish girl, you shall try your skill with hers."

Both went quickly to work and for hours their shuttles flew swiftly in and out.

Athena, as usual, used the sky for her loom and in it she wove a picture too beautiful to describe.

If you wish to know more about it look at the western sky when the sun is setting.

Arachne's work, though her colors were in harmony and her weaving wonderfully fine, was full of spite and selfishness.

When the work was finished Arachne lifted her eyes to Athena's work. Instantly she knew that she had failed.

Ashamed and miserable she tried to hang herself in her web.

Athena saw her and said in pity, "No, you shall not die; live and do the work for which you are best fitted.

"You shall be the mother of a great race which shall be called spiders.

"You and your children shall be among the greatest spinners and weavers on earth."

As she spoke, Arachne became smaller and smaller until she was scarcely larger than a fly.

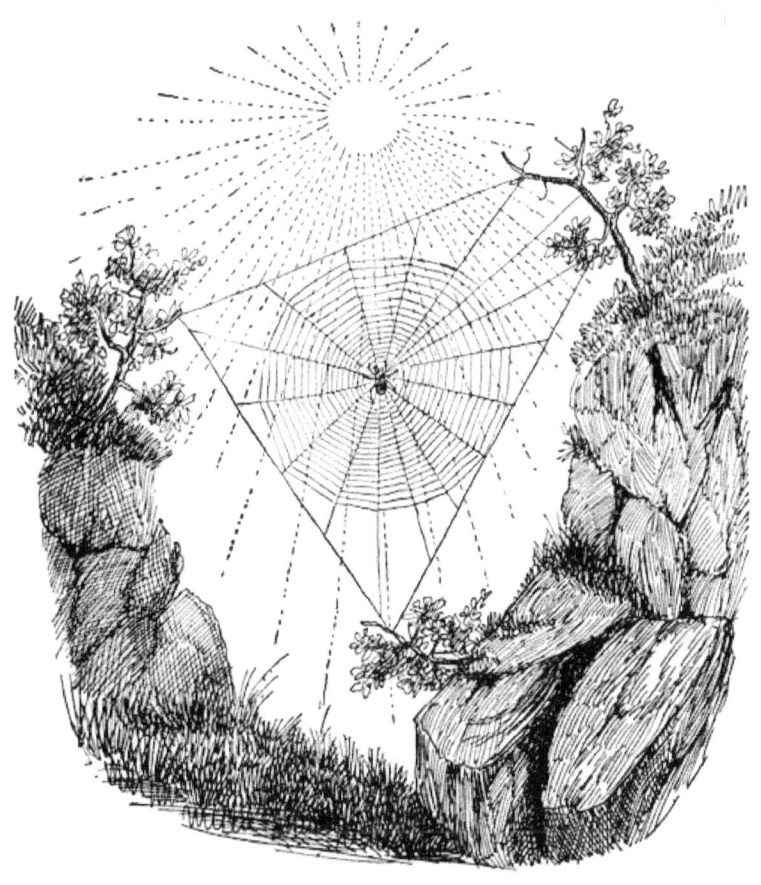

From that day to this Arachne and her family have been faithful spinners, but they do their work so quietly and in such dark places, that very few people know what marvelous weavers they are.

# AURORA AND TITHONUS.

THE beautiful youth, Tithonus, loved Aurora, the queen of the dawn. He was the first one to greet her each day as she drew back the purple curtains of the east.

He made his bed on the green grass in the meadow that he might not miss her coming.

Aurora grew to expect his welcome and to love the youth dearly.

One morning when she came Tithonus was not in his usual place.

As she looked anxiously around she saw him with pale face and closed eyes lying upon the ground.

She darted down to earth and carried his almost lifeless body to Zeus.

She begged the great king to promise that Tithonus should never die.

But alas, in her haste, she forgot to ask that he might forever remain young. Therefore he grew old and bent, and could no longer walk.

In misery, he begged to go back to the cool grass in the meadow where he had been so happy.

Aurora in pity said, "you shall go, my Tithonus. To make you happy is my dearest wish.

"You shall be free from all care.

"You shall not be a man, lest you be compelled to work for your food in your old age.

"You shall be a grasshopper, free to dance in the meadow grass all the long summer days.

"I have prepared a dress for you, which shall protect you well."

Then she gave Tithonus the wonderful grasshopper coat of mail which had been unknown on earth until this time.

She tinted it a soft green so that he might not be noticed in the grass.

Tithonus went that day to live in the meadow and there, any summer day, you may find him and his family hopping merrily about in the sunshine.

# HOW THE ROBIN'S BREAST
# BECAME RED.

ONG ago in the far North, where it is very cold, there was only one fire.

A hunter and his little son took care of this fire and kept it burning day and night. They knew that if the fire went out the people would freeze and the white bear would have the Northland all to himself. One day the hunter became ill and his son had the work to do.

For many days and nights he bravely took care of his father and kept the fire burning.

The white bear was always hiding near, watching the fire. He longed to put it out, but he did not dare, for he feared the hunter's arrows.

When he saw how tired and sleepy the little boy was, he came closer to the fire and laughed to himself.

One night the poor boy could endure the fatigue no longer and fell fast asleep.

The white bear ran as fast as he could and jumped upon the fire with his wet feet, and rolled upon it. At last, he thought it was all out and went happily away to his cave.

A gray robin was flying near and saw what the white bear was doing.

She waited until the bear went away. Then she flew down and searched with her sharp little eyes until she found a tiny live coal. This she fanned patiently with her wings for a long time.

Her little breast was scorched red, but she did not stop until a fine red flame blazed up from the ashes.

Then she flew away to every hut in the Northland.

Wherever she touched the ground a fire began to burn.

Soon instead of one little fire the whole north country was lighted up.

The white bear went further back into his cave in the iceberg and growled terribly.

He knew that there was now no hope that he would ever have the Northland all to himself.

This is the reason that the people in the north country love the robin, and are never tired of telling their children how its breast became red.

# AN INDIAN STORY OF THE ROBIN.

HEN an Indian boy was eleven years old, he was sent into a forest far away from his home.

He had to stay there all alone and fast for seven days and nights.

The Indians thought that at this time a spirit came into the youth which helped him to become a great chief and warrior.

The spirit also told the boy what his name should be in the tribe.

Once there was a fierce Indian war chief who had only one son.

The little boy was not strong, but his father loved him more than anything else on earth.

When this boy was eleven years old, the chief went out into the forest and built a small lodge for him to stay in.

In it he placed a mat of reeds which his good squaw had woven with great care.

By the side of the mat he laid a bow, some arrows and his own great tomahawk.

Next he painted pictures upon the trees along the path leading from the wigwam to the lodge.

He did this that the little boy might easily find his way home.

When everything was ready he sadly sent his son away into the forest.

He missed him so much that he went every morning to look at him.

Each day he asked him if the spirit had not come to him.

Each day the little boy shook his head without opening his eyes.

On the fifth day his son said to him, "Father, take me home or I shall die. No spirit will come to me."

The old chiefs pride was greater than his pity and he said, "No, my son, you must not be a coward. You shall be as wise as a fox and as strong as a bear.

"Better that you should die than that boy and squaw should cry 'Shame' upon your father's son.

"Be patient, I will come in two days and bring you food."

The sixth day came and the little boy lay upon the mat white and still.

On the seventh, when the chief came with the sun's first rays, his son was not in the lodge nor about it.

Above the door sat a bird with brown coat and red breast, which until this time had been unknown to man.

Sadly the chief listened to the bird and understood its message.

"Mourn me not, great chief," it sang. "I was once your son.

"I am happy now and free.

"I am the friend of man and shall always live near him and be his companion.

"I shall bring the tidings of spring.

"When the maple buds shoot and the wild flowers come, every child in the land shall know my voice.

"I shall teach how much better it is to sing than to slay.

> "Chief, listen, chief,
> Be more gentle; be more loving.
> Chief, teach it, chief,
> Be not fierce, oh, be not cruel;
> Love each other!
> Love each other!"

# THE RED-HEADED WOODPECKER.

**T**HERE was an old woman who lived on a hill. You never heard of any one smaller or neater than she was. She always wore a black dress and a large white apron with big bows behind.

On her head was the queerest little red bonnet that you ever saw.

It is a sad thing to tell, but this woman had grown very selfish as the years went by.

People said this was because she lived alone and thought of nobody but herself.

One morning as she was baking cakes, a tired, hungry man came to her door.

"My good woman," said he, "will you give me one of your cakes? I am very hungry. I have no money to pay for it, but whatever you first wish for you shall have."

The old woman looked at her cakes and thought that they were too large to give away. She broke off a small bit of dough and put it into the oven to bake.

When it was done she thought this one was too nice and brown for a beggar.

She baked a smaller one and then a smaller one, but each one was as nice and brown as the first.

At last she took a piece of dough only as big as the head of a pin; yet even this, when it was baked, looked as fine and large as the others.

So the old woman put all the cakes on the shelf and offered the stranger a dry crust of bread.

The poor man only looked at her and before she could wink her eye he was gone.

She had done wrong and of course she was unhappy.

"Oh, I wish I were a bird!" said she, "I would fly to him with the largest cake on the shelf."

As she spoke she felt herself growing smaller and smaller until the wind whisked her up the chimney.

She was no longer an old woman but a bird as she had wished to be. She still wore her black dress and red bonnet. She still seemed to have the large white apron with the big bows behind.

Because from that day she pecked her food from the hard wood of a tree, people named this bird the red-headed wood-pecker.

# THE STORY OF THE

# PUDDING STONE.

NCE upon a time a family of giants lived upon the high mountains in the West.

One day the mother giant was called away from home.

She arose early in the morning and made ready the bread and butter for the little giants to eat while she was gone.

When she had finished her work it was not yet time to start upon her journey.

She said to herself, "My children are the best children in the world and they shall have a treat. I have many plums left from the Christmas feast. I will make them a plum pudding for a surprise.

The good woman brought together the plums which it had taken her many days to prepare with the help of all her children. Indeed she had emptied several mountain lakes to get water enough to wash them all.

She now mixed these wonderful plums into a pudding and put it into an oven to bake.

The mixing took so long that she had to hurry, and she quite forgot to say anything about the pudding to the little giants.

She had intended to tell them about it just before she left them.

It was afternoon when the giant children found the pudding.

It was badly burned upon the top by that time.

They had already eaten the bread and butter and were not hungry.

One little giant said to the others, "Let us make balls of the pudding and see who can throw the farthest."

You know that giants are very strong, and away went the pudding up into the air.

The little giants made little balls and the older giants threw pieces as big as a house.

Many pieces went over the mountains and fell down into the valley beyond.

Indeed this wonderful pudding was scattered for miles over the whole land, for the giants did not stop throwing as long as there was any pudding left in the pan.

When the sun had shone upon it many days and dried and hardened it, people called it pudding stone.

You may find it to-day thrown all over the land, full of the plums which the good woman washed with the waters of many lakes.

# STORY OF SISYPHUS.

ITTLE White Cloud was the Ocean's daughter. The Ocean loved her, and wished always to keep her near him.

One day, when her father was asleep, White Cloud went out to walk alone.

The Sun saw her and said, "Come, White Cloud, I am your king, I will give you a ride upon my bright rays." White Cloud had often longed for this very thing, so she went gladly, and soon found herself among the fleecy clouds in the sky.

When the Ocean awoke he called his little daughter. She did not answer. He called again and again, louder and still louder, until the people said, "Listen, it is thundering!"

But the Ocean only heard the echo of his own voice from the shore. He rushed high up on the beach and moaned aloud.

He ran into all the caves but White Cloud could not be found.

Every one had loved White Cloud, so by this time all the water was white with the crests of the weeping sea nymphs.

A great giant was sitting upon the shore near the sea. His name was Sisyphus. He felt sorry for the Ocean and said, "Listen, friend Ocean, I often watch you carrying the great ships and wish that I, too, had a great work to do.

"You see how dry it is on this side of the mountain. Few people come this way. You are not even now as lonely as I, yet I want to help you. Promise me that you will put a spring upon this

35

mountain side, where all the tired and thirsty people may drink, and I'll tell you where White Cloud is."

The Ocean said, "I cannot put a spring upon the mountain, but if you will follow my son, River, he will take you to a spring where he was born."

The giant told the Ocean how the Sun ran away with White Cloud. The Sun heard him and was angry. He placed Sisyphus in the sea saying, "You are far too strong to sit idly here upon the shore. You say you want a great work to do; you shall have it. You shall forever use your strength to push these stones upon the shore, and they shall forever roll back upon you."

The giant began his work at once, and has worked faithfully every day since that time.

Many people do not yet know what his work is. Do you? Do you know what Sisyphus is making?

# THE PALACE OF ALKINOÖS.

 N a high plain covered with flowers once lived good King Alkinoös and his gentle people, the Phaiakians.

They were great sailors and went about in silver ships without rudders or sails.

These wonderful ships went slowly or very fast just as the sailors wished.

For many years the Phaiakians were peaceful and happy.

Though they were as brave as they were gentle, they hated war.

Far below the Phaiakians, in a valley, lived a people larger, darker, fiercer than themselves.

These dark people cared for nothing so much as war and conquest.

When they saw the silver ships with the golden prows, they wanted them for their own.

They armed themselves and made ready for a great battle.

To be sure of victory, they borrowed the thunder and lightning from Zeus.

The day came and all was ready for the dark people to advance.

They reached the land of the Phaiakians in the morning and King Alkinoös came forward to meet them.

They soon saw that he alone was more powerful than their entire army.

He was dressed in armor so bright that it dazzled their eyes to look at it. It was covered with millions of golden arrows tipped with diamonds. The king showed the frightened people how he could shoot the arrows in all directions at the same time.

The dark people trembled with fear, but King Alkinoös smiled at them, and then he and his people sailed slowly away toward the West.

On and on they went, until they came to a great silver sea.

Here they stopped and built a palace for their king.

This palace was made of silver and gold and precious stones.

Its towers were rose color and shone with a wonderful light.

Its steps were of pure gold.

On each side of the silver gates were huge dogs which guarded the palace.

There were boys in the halls dressed in white, holding burning torches.

There were girls weaving wonderful curtains and painting pictures upon the walls.

There were mountains and fountains, and rivers and lakes.

There were singing birds and flower gardens, and little children everywhere.

Even to this day, the great king often sits in his palace in the West when his day's work is done.

He loves to see the people glide about upon the silver sea, in their ships without rudders or sails.

The fierce, dark people still go to war.

They seldom let the gentle king see them fighting.

Yet often after a brave battle, Alkinoös comes out of his palace and smiles brightly upon them. The dark people blush and seem to smile at the king.

You must find out how much good these dark people do and how the King of the Phaiakians helps them in their work, if you wish to understand their friendship.

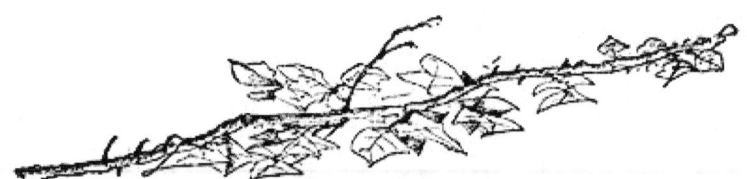

# PHAETHON.

PHAETHON was the son of Helios, who drove the chariot of the sun. He lived with his mother, the gentle Clymene, in a beautiful valley in the east.

One day when Phaethon was telling his companions about his father, the sky king, they laughed and said, "How do you know that Helios is your father? You have never seen him. If, as you say, he cannot safely come nearer to the earth, why do you not sometimes go to his land."

Phaethon answered, "My father's throne is far away from this valley. My mother has promised that when I am stronger, I shall go to my father's palace. I often watch his golden chariot roll by in its path and think perhaps some day I shall drive the glorious horses of the sun.

"I shall go now to my mother, and ask her how much longer I must wait."

When Phaethon told his mother what his companions had said she answered, "Go, my child, ask Great Helios if you are his son. If you are worthy to be the son of Helios you will be given strength and courage for the journey."

Phaethon gladly and bravely climbed the unused path which led to the palace of the sun.

At last he came in sight of the throne. He had never seen anything so beautiful. On one side were standing the days, months and the old years. On the other side were the seasons; Spring, covered with flowers; Summer, with her baskets of fruit and grain;

Autumn, in a many-colored dress; and Young Winter, with a crown of icicles.

As Phaethon came nearer to the throne, the light was greater than his eyes could bear. Its wonderful colors dazzled him.

Helios saw the brave youth and knew that it was Phaethon, his son. He took his glittering crown from his head and went forward to meet him.

Phaethon cried, "Great Helios, if you are my father give me and others proof that it is so."

Helios took him in his arms and kissed him. "You are indeed my son," he said. "I will put an end to your doubts. Ask any gift you will, and it shall be yours."

Phaethon had always had one wish in his heart and said, "O, my father, let me drive the wonderful golden chariot of the sun for just one day."

Helios shook his head sadly and said, "That is the one thing which you must not ask to do.

"You are my son, and I love you. For your own sake, I cannot let you do this. You have neither the strength nor the wisdom for the great work.

"The first part of the way is very steep and rugged. In the middle part, even I dare not look below at the far stretching earth, and the last part is full of terrible dangers."

Phaethon would not listen, but threw his arms around his father's neck and begged to go.

Helios said at last, "If you persist, foolish boy, you shall have your wish, for I cannot break my promise. I beg of you choose more wisely. Ask the most precious thing on earth or in the sky, and you shall have it."

Already Dawn had drawn back the purple curtains of the morning and the Hours were harnessing the horses to the chariot.

The stars and moon were retiring for the day.

The chariot glittered with jewels which sent the light in all directions. Phaethon looked upon it with delight and longed impatiently for the great joy of driving it.

Helios said, "O, my dear son, go not too high or you will scorch the dwelling of heaven, nor too low, lest you set the world on fire.

"Keep the middle path; that is best, and do not use the whip; rather, hold the horses in."

Phaethon was too happy to hear what his father was saying.

He leapt into the golden chariot and stood erect as the fiery horses sprang forth from the eastern gates of Day.

They soon missed the strong steady hand of their master.

Up, up they went, far into the sky, above the stars, and then plunged downward toward the earth.

The clouds smoked, the mountain tops caught fire, many rivers dried up and whole countries became deserts.

Great cities were burning, and even Poseidon cried out in terror from the sea.

Then the people on earth learned with what great wisdom the path of the sun was planned.

Helios saw that the whole world would soon be on fire, and cried to father Zeus to save the earth from the flames.

Zeus searched all the heavens for clouds and hurled his thunderbolts from the sky.

Phaethon fell from the chariot, down, down into a clear river.

The naiads cooled his burning brow, and gently sang him to sleep.

His sisters came to the banks of the river and wept.

That they might be always near Phaethon, Zeus, in pity changed them into poplar trees, and their tears became clear amber as they fell into the water.

At last the tired horses became quiet, and the great car rolled slowly back into its old path.

But the deserts and barren mountain tops still tell the story of the day Phaethon tried to drive the chariot of the sun.

# THE GRATEFUL FOXES.

T was springtime in Japan, and the blossoms hung thick on the cherry trees.

Butterflies and dragon flies fluttered over the golden colza flowers in the fields.

The rice birds chirped merrily. Everything seemed to say, "How good it is to live in days like these."

A beautiful princess, O Haru San, sat on the bank of a stream gaily pulling the lilies.

All the maidens of her court were with her.

Along the river bank came a troop of noisy, laughing boys, carrying a young cub fox. They were trying to decide who should have its skin and who its liver.

At a safe distance from them, in a bamboo thicket, father fox and mother fox sat looking sadly after their little cub.

The princess' heart was filled with pity, and she said:

"Boys, pray loose the little fox. See his parents weeping in the rocks."

The boys shook their heads.

"We shall sell the fox's skin," they said. "The liver, too, if well powdered, will be used to cure fevers in the fall."

"Listen," cried O Haru San, "It is springtime, and everything rejoices. How can you kill such a small soft beast?

"See, here is twice your price; take it all," and she drew copper money and silver money from her girdle.

The boys placed the little frightened animal in her lap and ran away, pleased to be so rich.

The cub felt the touch of her soft hand, and trembled no longer. She loosened carefully the knot and noose and string.

She stroked the red fur smooth again, and bound up the little bleeding leg. She offered it rice and fish to eat, but the black eyes plainly said, "This is very nice, but I hear my parents grieving near yonder beanstraw stack. I long to go and comfort them."

She set the little fox gently on the ground, and, forgetting its wounded leg, it leaped through the bushes at one happy bound.

The two old foxes gravely looked it over neck and breast.

They licked it from its bushy tail to its smooth, brown crown. Then, sitting up on their haunches, they gave two sharp barks of gratitude.

That was their way of saying, "We send you thanks, sweet maid."

As she walked home by the river side, all the world seemed more beautiful to O Haru San.

The summer time came and the blossoms upon the cherry trees became rich, ripe fruit. But there was no joy in the emperor's house.

His daughter, the gentle O Haru San, was ill. She grew paler and weaker each day. Physicians came from far and near, and shook their wise heads gravely.

When the emperor's magician saw her, he said, "No one can heal such sickness. A charm falls upon her every night which steals away her strength. He alone can break the spell, who, with sleepless eyes, can watch beside her bedside until sunrise."

Gray haired nurses sat by her until morning, but a deep sleep fell upon them at midnight.

Next fourscore maidens of the court, who loved her well, kept bright lights burning all the night, yet they, too, fell asleep.

Five counselors of state watched with her father at the bedside. Though they propped their eyes open with their fingers, yet in the middle of the night slumber overcame them.

All believed that the gentle maid must die.

The emperor was in despair, but Ito, a brave soldier, said, "I shall not sleep; let me one night guard the sweet O Haru San."

Her father led him to the chamber. Just at midnight Ito felt his eyes grow heavy.

He rose and held his sword above his head. "Rather will I die than sleep," he said.

Then came a great struggle. Often his head nodded, but by his love and strength Ito conquered sleep.

Suddenly he heard a voice which said, "Grate foxes' livers in the princess' rice broth and all her ills will disappear."

The next morning the hunters searched far and near for foxes. They knew that to the emperor a fox was worth its weight in gold. All day and night they were in the woods without food or rest.

At last they came sadly back to their homes. They brought no fox.

"All the foxes know," they said, "and have hidden themselves away."

The emperor in grief and anger cried, "Must my child perish? Shall a princess die for the lack of one poor fox?

"She was never willing that one should be slain and this is her reward."

Ito said, "I will get the fox." He started out with knife and net to seek it.

At the entrance of the town he met a woman dressed in strange garments. Very small and stooped she seemed to Ito. She carried a jar in her arms. She bowed low before Ito, and said, "What you seek is in the jar. I have brought it from afar."

"Here is gold," said Ito. "What is the price?"

The woman pulled the blue hood farther over her face and said, "Another time will do, I can wait. Hasten now to the princess."

Gladly Ito obeyed.

They made the broth in a bowl of beaten gold and fed it to O Haru San.

Immediately she was well and all was joy in the emperor's house.

The emperor said, "Ito, is she, who brought this blessing, paid?"

Ito answered, "Yonder she waits at the entrance of the town."

The emperor himself in his great joy went with Ito to meet her.

But they found only a dog-fox dead.

Around his neck they read this message, "This is my husband here.

"For his child he gives his liver to the princess, dear. I, his very lowly wife, have brought it."

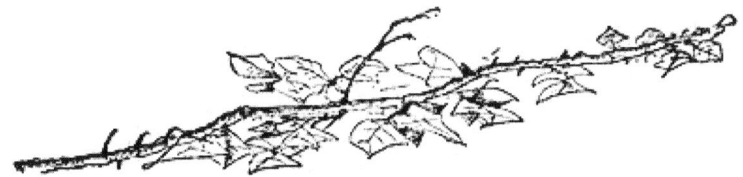

# PERSEPHONE.

EMETER had the care of all the plants, fruits and grains in the world.

She taught the people how to plow the fields and plant the seeds.

She helped them gather in their harvests.

They loved the kind earth-mother and gladly obeyed her.

They also loved her daughter, the beautiful Persephone.

Persephone wandered all day in the meadows among the flowers.

Wherever she went the birds, singing merrily, flocked after her.

The people said, "Where Persephone is, there is the warm sunshine.

"Flowers bloom when she smiles.

"Listen to her voice; it is like a bird's song."

Demeter wished always to have her child near her.

One day Persephone went alone into a meadow near the sea. She had made a wreath for her hair, and gathered all the flowers that her apron could hold.

Far away across the meadow she saw a white flower gleaming. She ran to it and found that it was a narcissus, but far more beautiful than any she had ever seen.

On a single stem were a hundred blossoms. She tried to pick it, but the stem would not break. With all her strength she grasped it, and slowly it came up by the roots.

It left a great opening in the earth which grew larger and larger.

Persephone heard a rumbling like thunder under her feet. Then she saw four black horses coming toward her from the opening.

Behind them was a chariot made of gold and precious stones.

In it sat a dark, stern man. It was Hades.

He had come up from his land of darkness, and was shading his eyes with his hands.

He saw Persephone, beautiful with flowers, and instantly caught her in his arms and placed her in the chariot beside him.

The flowers fell from her apron. "Oh! my pretty flowers," she cried, "I have lost them all."

Then she saw the stern face of Hades.

Frightened, she stretched out her hands to kind Apollo who was driving his chariot overhead. She called to her mother for help.

Hades drove straight toward his dark underground home.

The horses seemed to fly.

As they left the light, Hades tried to comfort Persephone.

He told her of the wonders of his kingdom. He had gold and silver and all kinds of precious stones.

Persephone saw gems glittering on every side as they went along, but she did not care for them.

Hades told her how lonely he was, and that he wished her to be his queen and share all his riches.

Persephone did not want to be a queen. She longed only for her mother and the bright sunshine.

Soon they came to the land of Hades.

It seemed very dark and dismal to Persephone, and very cold, too.

A feast was ready for her, but she would not eat.

She knew that any one who ate in Hades' home could never return to earth again.

She was very unhappy, though Hades tried in many ways to please her.

Everything on the earth was unhappy, too.

One by one the flowers hung their heads and said, "We cannot bloom, for Persephone has gone." The trees dropped their leaves and moaned, "Persephone has gone, gone."

The birds flew away and said, "We cannot sing for Persephone has gone."

Demeter was more miserable than any one else. She had heard Persephone call her, and had gone straight home.

She searched all the earth for her child. She asked every one she met these questions, "Have you seen Persephone? Where is Persephone?"

The only answer she ever received was, "Gone, gone, Persephone is gone!"

Demeter became a wrinkled old woman. No one would have known that she was the kind mother who had always smiled on the people.

Nothing grew on the earth and all was dreary and barren.

Demeter said that she would do nothing until Persephone returned to her.

It was useless for the people to plow the soil.

It was useless to plant the seeds. Nothing could grow without the help of Demeter.

All the people were idle and sad.

When Demeter found no one on earth who could tell her about Persephone, she looked up toward the sky. There she saw Apollo in his bright chariot. He was not driving as high in the sky as he was wont to do.

Often he gathered dark mists about him so that none saw him for many days.

Demeter knew that he must know about Persephone, for he could see all things on earth and in the sky.

Apollo told Demeter that Hades had carried Persephone away and that she was with him in his underground home.

Demeter hastened to the great father Zeus, who could do all things.

She asked him to send to Hades for her daughter. Zeus called Hermes. He bade him go as swiftly as the wind to the home of Hades. Hermes whispered to everything on the way that he was going for Persephone so that all might be ready to welcome her back.

He soon arrived in the kingdom and gave Hades the message from Zeus. He told about the barren earth and of how Demeter was mourning for her child. He said she would not let anything grow until Persephone came back. The people must starve if she did not soon return.

Then Persephone wept bitterly, for that very day she had eaten a pomegranate and swallowed six of its seeds.

Hades pitied her and said that she need only stay with him one month for each seed she had eaten.

Joy gave her wings, and as swiftly as Hermes himself, Persephone flew up into the sunshine.

Apollo saw her and rose higher and higher into the sky. A gentle breeze came rustling from the southeast, and whispered something to everything he met.

Suddenly the flowers sprang up; the birds flocked together and sang; the trees put on bright green leaves.

Everything, great and small, began to say in his own language, "Be happy for Persephone has come! Persephone has come!"

Demeter saw these changes and was puzzled. "Can the earth be ungrateful? Does she so soon forget Persephone?" she cried.

It was not long however before her own face became beautiful and happy, for she held again her beloved child in her arms.

When Demeter found that Persephone could stay with her only half the year, she brought out the choicest treasures from her storehouse and while Persephone stayed, the world was filled with beauty and joy.

When she had gone, Demeter covered the rivers and lakes, and spread a soft white blanket over the sleeping earth.

Then she, too, fell asleep and dreamed such pleasant dreams that she did not awake until she felt Persephone's warm kiss on her forehead.

# THE SWAN MAIDENS.

A LONG, long time ago there was born in the east a wonderful king.

He was called "The King of the Golden Sword."

Every day he came in his golden chariot scattering heat, light and happiness among his people.

Every day he passed from his palace in the east far over to his throne in the west.

He never missed a day for he wanted to see that everyone had a full share of his gifts.

Throughout the kingdom the birds sang and the flowers bloomed. The sky was full of beautiful pictures which were constantly changing.

The king had many daughters who were called swan maidens.

They were as graceful as swans and usually wore white featherlike dresses.

The swan maidens loved their good father and each one longed to help him in his work.

Sometimes the king saw that the grass was brown or the buds were not coming out.

Then he called the swan maidens to him and said, "My children, this must not be. There is nothing more beautiful in the kingdom than the green grass and the trees. They need your care."

Gladly each maiden changed her dress and set out at once on her journey. Often they could not all work upon the grass and the buds.

Some of them ran off to play with the stones in the brook. The best ones went down to feed the roots and worms, and worked out of sight.

When their tasks were finished they always hurried back to their father, the king.

They went so noiselessly and swiftly that for a long time their way of travelling was a mystery.

In the fall, the king called the bravest swan maidens to him. He told them they must go away for a long time.

The swan maidens wrapped themselves in white, feathery blankets and came softly down to the shivering flowers.

Gently they placed a white spread on the earth and left no small seed uncovered.

At last, when the king smiled and their work was done, they stole away so softly and happily that no one missed them.

# THE POPLAR TREE.

 NE night, just at sunset, an old man found the pot of gold which lies under the end of the rainbow.

His home was far beyond the dark forest, through which he was passing.

The pot of gold was heavy, and he soon began to look for a safe place in which to hide it until morning.

A poplar tree stood near the path stretching its branches straight out from the trunk.

That was the way the poplar trees grew in those days.

"Ah," said the man, "This tree is the very place in which to conceal my treasure.

"The trees are all asleep, I see, and these leaves are large and thick."

He carefully placed the pot of gold in the tree, and hurried home to tell of his good fortune.

Very early the next morning, Iris, the rainbow messenger, missed the precious pot of gold.

She hastened to Zeus and told him of the loss.

Zeus immediately sent Hermes in search of it.

Hermes soon came to the forest where it was hidden.

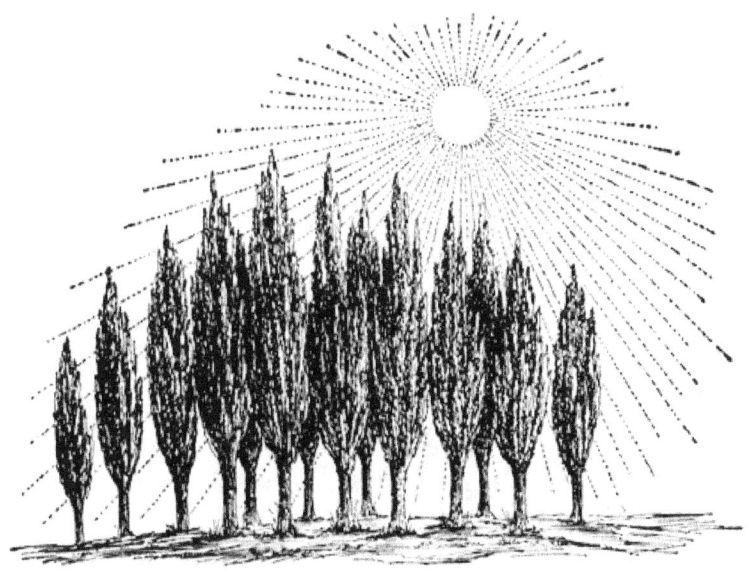

He awakened the trees, and asked them if they had seen the pot of gold.

They shook their heads sleepily, and murmured something which Hermes could not understand.

Then Zeus himself spoke to them. "Hold your arms high above your heads," he said, "that I may see that all are awake."

Up went the arms, but alas, down to the ground came the pot of gold.

The poplar tree was more surprised than any one else.

He was a very honest tree and for a moment hung his head in grief and shame. Then again he stretched his arms high above his head, and said, "Forgive me, great father; hereafter I shall stand in this way that you may know that I hide nothing from the sun, my king."

At first the poplar tree was much laughed at.

He was often told that he looked like a great umbrella which a storm had turned inside out.

But as years went by every small poplar was taught to grow as fearless, straight and open hearted as himself, and the whole poplar family became respected and loved for its uprightness and strength.

Merriman Co.,

# THE DONKEY AND THE SALT.

NE time a merchant went to the seashore for a load of salt.

There were many hills and streams to cross on the journey.

As the path was narrow and rocky, the man made his donkey carry the salt in large bags upon his back. It was a warm day, and the donkey did not like his heavy load.

He hung down his head and went as slowly as he could.

After a while they came to a stream which had only a foot bridge over it.

The donkey went through the water, splash! splash! splash! In the middle of the stream was a large stone which he did not see.

He stumbled and fell, and the water ran over the bags of salt.

Soon the donkey was glad that he had fallen, for he found his load much lighter.

They came to another stream, but the donkey did not stumble this time. He lay down in the middle of the brook.

He was a wise donkey.

This time he lost so much salt that his master was angry, for he was obliged to go back to the seashore for another load.

As they were walking along, the merchant laughed to himself.

He thought he knew a way to cure the donkey of this trick.

When they came to the seashore, he filled the bags with sponges, and started for home.

The donkey thought, "What a light load I have," and trotted gaily along over the rough road.

Again they came to the brook. "Ah!" thought the donkey, "I will make my load still lighter."

He lay down in the middle of the brook.

This time he found his load so heavy that he could scarcely rise.

His master kindly helped him, but the donkey was not happy.

The water ran down his sides and made him more miserable.

"Oh," thought he, "I will never lie down in the water again."

Once more his master led him back to the seashore.

He filled the bags with salt.

The donkey was wiser now and carried the salt safely home.

# THE SECRET OF FIRE.

## A TREE STORY.

 NE summer night a great army of pine trees settled down in a quiet valley to rest. They were a tall, dark, grave-looking company.

They held their heads high in the air, for they were the only trees in the world who knew the wonderful secret of fire.

High above this valley, on the hillside, lived a little company of oaks.

They were young, brave, and strong-hearted.

When they saw the great band of pines marching into the valley, the tallest one said:

"Let us make them divide the gift of fire with us."

"No," said the oldest, wisest oak, "we must not risk, foolishly, the lives of our acorns. We could do nothing against so many."

All the acorns had been listening to what the tree said. Each one longed to help in finding out the great secret.

One of them became so excited that he fell from the limb, down upon the hard ground. He did not stop at the foot of the tree, but rolled over and over, far down into the valley.

Here a brook picked him up and hurried him away; but as he stopped to rest by a stone, he heard his good friend, the wind, talking to a pine tree.

"What is the secret of fire which the pine trees know?" asked the wind. "Don't you think it is selfish to keep it all to yourselves?"

The pine tree loved the wind and answered:

"Great wind, it is, indeed, a wonderful secret; you must never tell it." Then she whispered it to the wind.

The little acorn went on and on down the stream.

He came to an old log, which was the home of a large family of squirrels. The mother squirrel was very sad. The last flood had brought her and her children far away from her old forest home. Her family had all been saved, but food was scarce and winter was near.

The acorn felt very sorry for her and said:

"I am too small to do you much good alone. If you will carry me back to my home, I will show you a forest with plenty of nuts. You can take your family there in the fall."

This the squirrel was very glad to do.

As they went along the acorn called to all the elms, maples, willows and hickories to meet that night on the hilltop.

"Come to the hill across from the great blue mountains," he said. "There you will learn the secret of fire."

By evening they were all there, in great companies, ready for war on the pines.

When the squirrel came to the forest and saw all the nuts she was much pleased.

She offered to carry the acorn to the very top of the tallest tree. The trees were all glad of this, for every one wanted to hear what he said.

When the acorn began to speak, even the wind stopped whispering and listened.

"Friends," he said, "there must be no battle. The pine trees have only the same gift of fire that you have. To every tree that stretches out its arms the glorious sun gives this gift. But it was in this way that the pine trees learned the secret of getting the fire from the wood: They saw an old Indian chief with two curious pieces of wood. One was round and smooth, the other was sharp-pointed. With all his strength he was rubbing them together. Soon he had worn a groove in the round stick. He rubbed faster and faster, and there in the groove was a tiny spark of fire. Then the Indian blew his breath upon the spark and a little yellow flame leaped up. All the pine trees saw it. 'See, it is fire!' they said."

When the great company of trees had heard the acorn's story they shook their heads in doubt. Then the acorn said:

"This is the true secret of fire. If you do not believe it why do you not try it for yourselves."

They took this advice and all the trees learned that what he had said was true.

They were so happy that they spent the whole night in singing and dancing.

In the morning, when they saw the great blue mountains and the beautiful valley, many of them settled down upon the hillside for life.

The pines looked up and saw hundreds of trees with their shining arms. They were so frightened that they climbed high up on the mountain side. There they stayed a long, long time.

They grew sad and lonely, and often sighed and wished for their old home and comforts. But they were brave and strong-hearted, and helped each other.

At last, some of them came down into the valley again. Through suffering they had grown strong and unselfish. They gave their best trees to the people and their fairest to the children at Christmas time.

Indeed, there is not a tree in the world to-day more loved than the pine tree, who first had the secret of fire.

# A FAIRY STORY.

OME fairies once lived in a dark glen in a pine forest.

They were real fairies, many of them not higher than a pin.

Their greatest treasure was a magic cap which had been in the fairy family for many generations.

The most wonderful thing about the cap was that it fitted exactly any one who wore it.

When one fairy put it on, he and all the others became invisible.

A stupid race of giants lived among the mountains near them. They wanted the fairy cap more than anything else in the world.

One warm day when the elves were away from home, a giant came into the glen. He was seeking just such a cool place for his afternoon nap.

He was so large and the glen so small that when he lay down he almost filled the valley.

The music of a fairy brook soon lulled him to sleep.

Perhaps you have heard how a giant snores, and how his breath comes in great puffs.

The giant was snoring and puffing when the fairies came towards home.

They heard the strange sound and thought a great storm was brewing.

"There has never been such a wind in the glen," said the fairy queen.

"We will not go down into it. We must seek shelter for to-night on this hillside."

Just then they came to the giant's ear.

"Here is a fine cavern," the queen said, and she stopped and waved her wand.

A fairy hastened forward to carry the cap to a safe place in the cave, for that was always their first care.

Just then the giant awoke.

He raised his great head.

Oh, how miserable the fairies were!

They wept and moaned until even the dull ear of the giant heard them.

It was a sound like the tolling of tiny silver bells.

He listened and understood what the wee voice of the prisoner in his ear was saying.

He was the wisest and most kind-hearted of all the giants.

He helped the little creature gently out into his hand, and looked at him in wonder.

He had never before seen a fairy.

In vain the brave little fellow tried to conceal the precious cap.

The giant saw the wonderful star and knew at once that he had the treasure cap of the elves.

He set the fairy carefully upon the ground, and shouted for joy as he found that the cap exactly fitted his own great head.

The poor fairies could no longer see him, but they heard a sound like thunder, as he hurried over the stones towards his home.

They were now afraid to move about while the sun shone.

They crept under leaves and into shells and cried bitterly.

By sundown every plant in the glen was wet with their tears.

The sharp eyes of the eagle on the mountain top saw them and a great pity filled his heart.

"I must help the fairies," he said, "otherwise I should not be worthy to be called the 'king of birds'."

He went directly to the home of the giants and demanded the cap, but they refused to give it up.

All that an eagle could do, he did, but as the giants wore the invisible cap he could not see them. He could only hear their great voices.

He knew however that the giants were proud of their great size and strength, and liked, above all things, to be seen.

He was sure that they would not wear the cap in battle, and he did not lose hope.

One day they carefully placed it under a large stone on the mountain side below them.

The keen eye of the eagle was watching.

He flew fearlessly to the spot as soon as the giants had left it.

He lifted the stone in his great talons, and was soon flying away with the cap to the fairy glen.

The giants saw him, and knew at once what he was doing.

They began a fierce attack upon him.

The air was filled with flying arrows and sharp rocks. Drops of blood fell on the mountain side, and many feathers fluttered down, but the brave eagle was soon out of their reach.

He did not stop until the cap was safe in the fairy queen's lap.

There was great rejoicing among the fairies that day.

They had a feast in the eagle's honor, and healed his wounds with fairy magic.

On the mountain side, wherever the blood and feathers fell, there sprang up trees with featherlike leaves and blood-red berries.

All the giants, fairies, plants and animals knew why they grew.

The unselfish love in the eagle's blood could not die, but lived again in the beautiful trees.

But people who did not know how they came there, called them mountain ash trees.

# PHILEMON AND BAUCIS.

 N a high hill in Greece, long ago, lived Philemon and Baucis. They had always been poor but never unhappy.

At the time of this story the people in the valley below them were very busy.

Zeus, their king, had sent word that he was about to visit them.

Hermes, his messenger, was to come with him.

The people were getting ready great feasts, and making everything beautiful for their coming. For miles out of the city, men were watching for the golden chariot and white horses of the king.

One night, just at dark, two beggars came into the valley.

They stopped at every house and asked for food and a place to sleep.

But the people were too busy or too tired to attend to their needs.

Footsore and weary, at last they climbed the hill to the hut of Philemon and Baucis.

These good people had eaten scarcely anything for several days that they might have food to offer the king.

When they saw the strangers, Philemon said, "Surely these men need food more than the king."

Baucis spread her one white table cloth upon the table.

She brought out bacon and herbs, wild honey and milk.

She set these before the strangers with all the good dishes that she had.

Then a wonderful thing happened.

The dishes which the strangers touched turned to gold.

The milk in the pitcher became rich nectar.

Philemon and Baucis dropped upon their knees.

They knew that their guests could be no other than Zeus and Hermes.

Zeus raised his hand and said, "Arise, good people, ask what you will and it shall be yours."

Philemon and Baucis cried in one voice:

"Grant, oh Zeus, that one of us may not outlive the other, but that both may die in the same instant."

This had long been the wish in each heart, and the fear of being left alone in the world was the one trouble of their old age.

Zeus smiled and changed their rude hut into a beautiful castle, and granted them many years of happy life.

One morning the people in the valley noticed that the castle had disappeared.

They hurried to the spot and found growing in its place two beautiful trees, an oak and a linden.

No trace of the good couple could be found.

Many years after, however, a traveller lying under the trees heard them whispering to each other.

He lay very still and soon learned that in them Philemon and Baucis still lived, happy and contented, and protected by Zeus from all harm.

# DAPHNE.

APHNE was the daughter of the River Peneus.

She was a beautiful child and her father loved her more than anything else in the world.

Her home was in a cave which he had cut for her in a great white cliff.

The walls of the cave were of marble.

From the roof hung crystal chandeliers which Peneus' servants had made.

On the floor was a soft green carpet woven by the water fairies.

Peneus brought his most beautiful pebbles to Daphne's cave every night.

He sang songs to her in the evenings and told her stories of his travels.

She visited with him the great island which he was building in the sea.

When the morning star shone in the sky it was Daphne who awakened the birds and flowers.

With her golden hair flying behind her, she sped into the forest. Everything awoke when they felt the touch of her rosy fingers, and smiled as they saw her happy face.

The trees and the forest animals were her playfellows, and she had no wish for other friends.

She learned their ways, and the deer could not run more swiftly than she, nor the birds sing more sweetly.

One day as she was running over the stones near the cave, King Apollo saw her.

"Ah, little maid," said he, "You are very beautiful. Your feet are too tender for the hard rocky earth.

"Come, you shall live with me in my palace in the sky."

But Daphne fled from him.

She did not want to leave her beautiful earth home.

Fear gave her wings, and faster and faster she flew.

Her hair streamed behind her like a cloud of golden light.

Apollo followed more swiftly than the wind.

"Stop and listen," he cried; "I am not a foe, foolish girl. It is Apollo who follows you. I shall carry you to a home more beautiful than anything you have ever seen."

She felt his breath upon her hair, and saw his hand as he stretched it forth to seize her.

"Father, save me from Apollo," she cried. "Let the earth enclose me."

Peneus heard her voice and instantly her feet became fastened in the soil like roots. A soft bark covered her body and her beautiful hair became the leaves of the laurel tree.

Apollo sadly gathered some of the leaves and wove them into a wreath. He laid his hand upon the tree and said, "I would have made you happy, but you would not listen to me.

"At least you shall be my tree. Your leaves shall be ever green, and heroes shall be crowned with them in sign of victory."

# AN INDIAN STORY

# OF THE MOLE.

N Indian once saw a squirrel sunning himself in a tree top.

The squirrel saw the hunter and leaped upon a passing cloud.

He had escaped into Cloudland before an arrow could reach him.

The Indian set a trap for him hoping that he would soon return to the tree for food.

The sun happened to be coming that way and was caught in the trap.

Suddenly, in the middle of the day, it became dark.

The Indian was frightened and said, "Ah me, what have I done, I have surely caught the sun in my trap."

He sent many animals up to set it free, but all were instantly burned to ashes.

At last the mole said, "Let me try, I shall bore through the ground of the sky and gnaw off the cords which hold the trap."

He did this, but just as he loosened the last cord the sun sprang forth and the bright light shone full in his eyes.

The poor mole dropped to the earth and though his friends were able to save his life, he was blind.

"You need not pity me," he said, "I prefer to live underground, where really there is no use for eyes."

All the moles were so proud of this hero mole that they tried to be like him in every way.

They, too, went to live in a dark hole in the earth.

Their eyes, which they did not need to use, became so small that they were entirely hidden by their fur. Indeed it is now so hard to find them that many people think the entire mole family is blind.

# HOW THE SPARK OF
# FIRE WAS SAVED.

 ONG ago when fire was first brought to earth, it was given into the care of two beldams at the end of the world.

The Cahroc Indians knew where it was hidden. They needed fire and were always planning ways to get it.

They went at last to the wise coyote.

"That is simple enough," said he, "I will show you a way to get it. Fire is a great blessing and should be free to all people."

The coyote knew every inch of the road to the beldams' hut.

Along the path leading to it, he stationed beasts, the strongest and best runners nearer the hut and the weaker ones farther off.

Nearest the guarded den, he placed one of the sinewy Cahroc men.

Then he walked boldly up to the door of the hut and knocked.

The beldams, not fearing a coyote in the least, invited him in.

They were often lonely, living so near the end of the world.

When the coyote had rested before the fire for some time, he said, "The Cahroc nation need fire. Could you not give them one small spark? You would never miss it. Here it is of no use."

The beldams answered, "We do not love it, but we dare not give it away. We must guard it while we live."

The coyote had expected them to say this.

He sprang to the window, and instantly outside were heard such sounds, that the beldams rushed out to see what the frightful noise could be.

Each animal in the line was sounding the watch-word of fire in his own way.

The wild horse neighed, the mountain lion roared, the gray wolf howled, the serpent hissed, the buffalo bellowed, and every small animal did its part equally well.

Indeed, it is no wonder that the beldams were frightened nearly to death.

The Cahroc man brought water and told them not to fear for themselves.

The coyote seized a half-burned brand and was off in an instant.

The beldams sprang after him and followed him closely over hill and valley. Faster than the wind they flew.

They were stronger than he, and though he put all his wild-wood nerve to the strain, they steadily gained.

Soon the race must end!

But Puma, the monstrous cat, was watching, and leaped up just in time to save the brand.

Each animal was in its place and the good fire passed on.

It came at last to the Cahroc nation, and was afterwards free to all people under the sun.

There were only two mishaps in all the race.

As the squirrel turned a corner of stumps and bowlders, his beautiful tail caught fire, and a brown track was burned up over his back to his shoulders, and the curl has remained in his tail to this day.

The frog had a harder fate.

He was the last one in the line of beasts. When the brand reached him it was smaller than the smallest coal in the grate.

He seized it carefully and jumped forward as fast as he could, but the hand of the foremost beldam caught him and held him fast.

How his heart beat!

His eyeballs bulged out of his head, and he has looked ever since much in the same scared way.

He did not lose his courage, however. He swallowed the coal and sprang into the water.

Sad to tell, the beldam still held in her hand his special pride and care, his tail.

Henceforth only the tadpoles could wear tails.

The frog sought a log and sat down upon it to think.

"I did my duty, even if I lost my beauty," he thought; "that is enough for a frog. This spark must be saved."

After much choking he spat the swallowed spark well into the bark.

The gift came, in this way, to all men; for, in even the wettest weather, if you rub two sticks together, fire is sure to come.

Because we know how the frog hurt his throat that day, we like to listen to his hoarse voice when we hear him singing to his children in the spring.

# BALDER.

HE people in the North once believed that high above the clouds was the beautiful plain of Asgard.

Odin, ruler of Asgard, mighty Thor, and many other heroes lived on the plain.

Their homes were great castles, splendid with silver and gold.

In the middle of the plain, and apart from the other dwellings, stood a pure white palace.

Nothing that was not fair and good had ever dared to enter it.

It was the home of Balder.

Because of his great beauty and wisdom, he was called "Balder the beautiful," and "Balder the good."

Everything loved him.

The dull rocks and the gray old mountains met him with a smile.

The flowers opened, the birds sang and the water sparkled when they saw his face.

One night he dreamed that he must soon leave Asgard and all the things that he loved.

The next night he dreamed that he was living in the gloomy underground world.

The third night, when the same terrible dream came to him, he was greatly troubled.

He told Odin, his father, and Frigga, his mother, about it.

Odin, in great fear, called together his wisest heroes.

They shook their heads but could do nothing to help him.

Frigga cried, "It shall not be! I, his mother, will save him."

She went straight way to Heimdal, who guarded the rainbow bridge.

Bifrost, which was the name of the bridge, was the only path which led from Asgard to the earth.

Heimdal allowed only those who lived in the plain to pass over it.

All feared Heimdal, yet they loved him.

He could see to the ends of the world.

He could hear the wool growing on the sheep's back, and knew when each grass blade broke into the sunshine.

Heimdal loved Balder and when he heard what troubled Frigga, pitied her. He gave her his swift black horse and showed her the way to the ends of the earth.

For nine days and nights she traveled without food or rest.

She asked everything she met to promise not to harm Balder.

Animals, flowers, trees, water, air, fire, everything she asked gladly gave the promise.

They smiled in wonder at the question.

Who could wish to hurt the gentle Balder?

Alas, the mistletoe did not promise.

Frigga saw it growing high up on an oak tree.

It seemed too small and weak to do any harm. She did not ask it to promise.

On the tenth day of her journey, she came back again to Asgard.

She told the sorrowing Odin and his friends what she had done.

In their joy they found a new way to do Balder honor.

He stood in their midst while the most skillful heroes hurled their arrows at him.

At first, they threw only small twigs and pebbles.

Everything, however, had soon proved itself true to its promise.

Then the heroes lost all fear of harming him and threw their warlike weapons.

Balder stood unharmed and smiling among them.

Each day they met on the plain and in this sport proved the love of all things for him.

The blind Höder was the only one in Asgard who could not join in the game.

He was Balder's brother and loved him very dearly.

Höder was not unhappy, but always cheered and shouted as gaily as the others.

One day as he stood alone, Loki saw him.

Loki was a mischief maker.

His jokes were often cruel; indeed, most of the unhappiness in Asgard was caused by Loki's unkindness.

"Höder, why do you not do Balder honor?" asked Loki.

"I am blind," Höder answered, "and besides I have nothing to throw."

"Here is my arrow," said Loki. "Take it; I will guide your hands."

Alas, the cruel Loki had made the arrow of mistletoe.

He knew that this was the only way in which Balder could be harmed.

He longed to see the surprise of the heroes when Balder should at last be wounded.

Away flew the arrow.

Balder, the beautiful, fell lifeless to the ground.

Then all Asgard was dark with sorrow.

Strong heroes wept and would not be comforted.

The earth grew cold, white and still.

The water would not flow, and the seeds refused to grow.

The birds were silent. No flowers breathed their perfumes into the air.

There was not a smile in all the world.

Odin said, "This cannot be.

"Balder shall return. I, myself, will go and bring him from Hela's dark regions."

But Frigga had already sent a messenger to the spirit world to beg Queen Hela to release Balder.

While waiting for the messenger to return, the heroes were not idle.

For twelve days and nights they worked as only love can make men work. They did not pause for food nor rest.

They built a great funeral pyre, and no one was too small to help in the work of love.

They found Balder's ship upon the seashore.

They brought great logs from the forest and bound them upon the deck.

Upon these they placed his beautiful white horse, his dogs, his shining armor, and many things which he had loved on earth.

When it was finished, they raised the sails, set the ship on fire and pushed it out upon the sea.

They sang and wept all night until at sunrise the sails fell.

They watched the flames die down and the waves wash over the sinking ship.

As they turned sadly from the shore, they met the messenger from Hela's regions.

"Rejoice," he said, "Hela says, 'If everything living and lifeless weep for Balder, he may return to us.'"

There was great happiness in Asgard that day.

"Surely," they thought, "everything in the world will weep for Balder."

They had forgotten the cruel Loki.

He sat with dry eyes though rocks and trees, birds and flowers, wind and clouds were shedding tears.

When Odin found that Balder could not return to life, his anger and grief were terrible to see.

In fear, Loki hid himself deep in the earth under a mountain.

Frigga knew that he was conquered, and she patiently waited for the time when Balder should again be allowed to bring gladness to the earth, and fill all the heavens with the glory of his smile.

# HOW THE CHIPMUNK GOT THE STRIPES ON ITS BACK.

DO you all know the little striped chipmunk which lives in our woods?

He has a cousin in far off India called the geloori.

It is said the stripes came on the back of the geloori in a wonderful way.

One day the great Shiva saw a little gray chipmunk on the seashore.

He was dipping his bushy tail into the sea, and shaking out the water on the shore.

Twenty times a minute he dipped it into the ocean.

In wonder, Shiva said, "What are you doing, little foolish, gray, geloori? Why do you tire yourself with such hard labor?"

The geloori answered, "I cannot stop, great Shiva.

"The storm blew down the palm tree, where I built my nest.

"See! the tree has fallen seaward, and the nest lies in the water; my wife and pretty children are in it; I fear that it will float away. Therefore all day and all night I must dip the water from the sea.

"I hope soon to bale it dry.

"I must save my darlings even if I spoil my tail."

Shiva stooped and with his great hand stroked the little squirrel.

On the geloori's soft fur from his nose to the end of his tail, there came four green stripes! They were the marks of Shiva's fingers, placed there as signs of love.

Shiva raised his hand, and the water rolled back from the shore. Safe among the rocks and seaweeds, the palm tree lay on dry land.

The little squirrel hastened to it; his tail was now high in the air. He found his wife and children dry and well in their house of woven grass-blades.

As they sang their welcomes to him, the geloori noticed with delight that each smooth little back was striped with marks of Shiva's fingers.

This sign of love is still to be seen upon the back of chipmunks.

That is the reason why in India, good men never kill them.

A man who loves both children and chipmunks says, when he tells this story, "Perhaps our squirrels, though Shiva never stroked them, would be grateful if we left them, unharmed, to play in the maples in our woods."

# THE FOX AND THE STORK.

FOX met a stork and invited him to dinner.

"With all my heart, friend," said the stork.

When they arrived at the home of the fox and dinner was served, he was not so happy.

The fox had fine hot soup, but he served it in shallow plates.

The poor stork could only stand by and watch the fox eat.

The fox seemed to think that it was a very good joke.

The next day the stork met the fox and invited him to dinner. The stork brought out fine hot soup in a high narrow necked bottle, but the fox could not see the joke at all.

The stork said, "Friend fox, enjoy your dinner. I hope that the soup is as well flavored as yours was yesterday."

As he said this he poured out half of the soup into a bowl and set it before the fox.

The cunning old fox felt so ashamed that he has never looked anyone straight in the face since that day.

# PROMETHEUS.

 REECE is far away to the east over a great ocean. It is a very small country with high mountains in every part of it.

The people who lived there long ago could not easily go from one place to another.

Some of the mountains reached above the clouds and made great walls around their homes. Men sometimes lived all their lives near the sea and never saw it.

These people who were shut up in the little valley of Greece did many wonderful things.

As they could not go far from their homes they had time to see how beautiful the things around them were.

Perhaps they looked at the sky so much that they wished to have everything on earth just as beautiful.

They gave their children work to do which made them strong and graceful.

Some of the Greeks carved statues from the marble in the mountains. Some built great temples of it.

Some painted pictures, while others made gardens more beautiful than pictures.

Others wrote books. Many of the stories you like were written by the poets who lived in Greece long ago.

In all these ways the Greeks showed their love for their country and made it a better place in which to live.

Though they were so wise they had many thoughts which seem strange to us.

They believed that long before they were born a race of giants had lived among the mountains.

At one time the giants grew angry with Zeus, their king, and wished to take his throne away from him.

There was a wise giant, named Prometheus, who begged them not to attempt to do this.

He tried to show them how foolish they were.

They would not listen to him. Zeus lived upon Mount Olympus, the highest mountain in Greece.

The giants brought great rocks to this mountain and piled them up, higher and higher, until they reached the sky.

Zeus waited until the giants had finished their work and were ready for battle.

Then he put out his hand and touched the great mound. Instantly it fell over into the sea.

Prometheus and his brother were now the only people on earth.

They were so lonely that Zeus told them to model some people from clay.

Prometheus made animals and men and Epimetheus, his brother, gave them gifts of courage, swiftness and strength.

To some he gave feathers and wings, to others fur and claws, and to others a hard shelly covering.

When he came to man he had no covering left.

Zeus said, "I will clothe man," and that is the reason his covering is so delicate and beautiful.

Prometheus' people could not breathe.

Zeus sent him to Æolus, the god of the winds, for help.

Æolus sent his strong son, North Wind, back with Prometheus.

When North Wind saw the people of clay he whistled with surprise.

He blew his breath upon them.

They turned as white as snow and began to breathe.

They were a cold people, however, and Prometheus did not love them.

He went to Æolus again and this time South Wind and the zephyrs came with him.

South Wind brought the people green grass and flowers and birds.

The zephyrs showed them how to laugh and cry and sing and dance.

But the people were stupid.

They lived like ants in dark caves.

Prometheus saw that there was only one thing which would help them.

That was *fire.*

Fire was the most precious thing Zeus had, and he kept it ever burning around his throne.

When Prometheus asked for fire Zeus was angry.

"I have already given too much to your people," he said. "Let them now help themselves."

Prometheus was sad, indeed.

He loved his people more than he did himself.

At last he said: "They shall have the fire. I will pay for it with my life."

He went straight to Zeus' throne and filled a ferule with it, and carried it to his people.

Then the people began to be wise.

He taught them to cook, and to build houses, and to sail their ships upon the ocean.

He showed them how to get rich ores from the mountains and prepare them for use.

They learned how to plow and to reap and to store up their food for the winter.

Zeus was angry with Prometheus.

He chained him to a rock on the top of a high mountain.

He sent a great bird each day to torment him.

Zeus said that he must stay there until he repented and returned the fire to heaven.

There Prometheus stayed and suffered for many burning summers and long, cold winters.

Sometimes he grew faint-hearted and wished to be free.

Then he looked down and saw how the fire was helping the people and how happy they were, and he grew strong again.

After many, many years, a Greek hero who was sailing over the mountain in a golden cup, saw Prometheus.

It was Hercules. He shot the bird with a golden arrow, unbound the chains and set the wise Prometheus free.

# HERMES.

 EOLUS was the father of all the winds, great and small.

Long ago, they all lived happily together in a dark cave near the sea.

On holidays, North Wind, South Wind, East Wind and West Wind and their faithful sisters, came home and told of their travels.

The whirlwinds performed their most wonderful feats, and the zephyrs sang their sweetest songs.

These holidays, however, did not come often.

There were no idle children in the family of Æolus.

They swept and dusted the whole world. They carried water over all the earth. They helped push the great ships across the ocean.

The smaller winds scattered the seeds and sprinkled the flowers, and did many other things which you may find out for yourselves.

Indeed, they were so busy that Æolus was often left alone in his dark home for several days at a time.

He was glad when one summer morning a baby came to the cave.

The baby's name was Hermes, but Æolus called him "Little Mischief," because he was so little and so full of tricks.

Zeus was Hermes' father and his mother was the beautiful Queen Maia. She was often called "Star of Spring," because people thought that wherever she stepped flowers sprang from under the snow.

Æolus loved Hermes dearly. He taught him many secrets which only the winds know.

Hermes was a wise baby and understood all that Æolus told him.

When he was only two days old he could run and whistle as well as North Wind.

One day while he was very young he climbed out of his cradle and ran down to the seashore.

There he found an old tortoise shell. He picked it up and put a row of holes along each edge of the shell.

Through these holes he wove some reeds which he found upon the seashore. Then he blew softly upon the reeds.

The birds heard such wonderful music that they stopped to listen. The leaves on the trees began to dance, and nodded to the flowers to keep still.

The waves on the shore caught the tune and have been singing it ever since.

Hermes had invented the lyre and brought a new kind of music into the world. He soon tired of his lyre and went back to his cradle in the cave.

As he lay there he could see a beautiful blue meadow with many white cows upon it.

Hermes knew that the cows belonged to his brother, King Apollo.

"What fun," thought he, "I will go and make the cows run."

Off he ran after them until he was tired and out of breath.

Then he drove them all backward into a cave, and fastened them in.

King Apollo soon missed the cows and searched all the meadow for them.

He traced them to the cave, but when he came closer to it, he found that all the tracks led from the opening, not into it.

Near the cave he saw an old man who told him that he had seen the cows.

He said that with them he had seen a baby with wings on his cap and heels.

Apollo knew at once that the baby was his brother, Hermes.

He went straight to the cave of Æolus. There was Hermes in his cradle playing with the shell just like any other baby.

Apollo was angry and commanded him to stop laughing and crowing and tell him where the white cows were.

Hermes only picked up the shell and breathed softly upon it.

Apollo forgot his anger and everything but the beautiful music. He took Hermes in his arms and kissed him and begged him to teach him his secret.

Hermes was glad to be so easily forgiven. He gave Apollo the lyre and taught him many ways to play upon it. Apollo was soon able to make even sweeter music than Hermes, and he afterwards became the god of music.

He was so thankful to Hermes for his gift that he gave him a wonderful rod called the caduceus.

Whatever Hermes touched with the rod became wise, loving and unselfish. One time he saw two hissing serpents about to spring at each other in fury.

He touched them with the caduceus. Instantly they twined themselves lovingly around the rod and never again left it.

Apollo also gave Hermes charge over all the cows in the blue meadow. Hermes loved the cows and often took them with him on his journeys.

He was a wild youth and a great traveler, and so it happens that in nearly all the countries of the world Hermes and his white cows have been seen.

# IRIS' BRIDGE.

N the sky where the amber tints are seen on the clouds, Iris was born.

She loved her home and all the beautiful things around her.

Perhaps she sailed in the moon's silver boat and knew why the stars kept twinkling.

Perhaps she feasted on sunshine and dew, and slept on the soft white clouds.

More than anything in her sky-home, Iris loved her grandfather, the stern old ocean.

When he was merry, and drove his white horses over the water, she was happy.

When he was troubled, and the sky grew dark and sad, she quietly slipped her hand into his.

Instantly he smiled, and became gentle again.

He longed always to keep her with him, but the Sun said:

"No, Iris belongs to both ocean and sky.

"Let her be the messenger between heaven and earth."

They placed golden wings upon her shoulders and made her a bridge of beautiful colors.

One end of the bridge they rested in the sky, but the other Iris could fasten to the earth with a pot of gold.

This was the way Iris' path was made:

The earth gave the tints of her fairest flowers, the sea brought great ribbons of silvery mist, the wind was the shuttle, the sky was the loom and the Sun himself was the weaver.

It is no wonder that the most beautiful thing in all the world is Iris' bridge, the rainbow.